Oliver Twist

Retold by

Stewart Ross

Illustrated by

Alex Paterson

ARCTURUS

For Evie Ross, with much love—SR.

For Arthur—AP.

ARCTURUS

This edition published in 2021 by Arcturus Publishing Limited
26/27 Bickels Yard, 151–153 Bermondsey Street,
London SE1 3HA

Writer: Stewart Ross
Illustrator: Alex Paterson
Designer: Jeni Child
Editor: Sebastian Rydberg
Art Director: Jessica Crass

ISBN: 978-1-78828-686-2
CH006279NT
Supplier 24, Date 1220, Print run 11023

Printed in Malaysia

Contents

CHAPTER 1
The Workhouse Boy

At the beginning of our story, almost two hundred years ago, a young woman is lying in the street. She is very pretty but also very poor and very sick. She is expecting a baby.

No one knows her name.

She is carried into a workhouse, the ugly building for poor people without a home. That night, she gives birth to

a baby boy—and dies. Her only jewels, a ring and locket, are stolen.

Poor little baby boy! His father had disappeared, and now he has no mother. In other words, he is an orphan. It is not a very happy start to life.

Mr. Bumble, the fat, bossy man running the workhouse, names the orphans born there. He does this in alphabetical order. Since he named the last baby "Swubble," beginning with S, the next has to begin with T—so he chooses "Twist." Oliver Twist.

For the first nine miserable years of his life, Oliver is cared for by a matron. To be honest, she doesn't care for him at all. He sleeps in a coal cellar, and she gives him just enough food to stay alive.

*

On his ninth birthday, Oliver was returned to the workhouse. There, he lived with other poor and wretched boys. Mr. Bumble did not send them to school. Instead, he gave them hard, boring work to do.

All day long, the boys sat taking apart old rope. Their fingers were red and raw. If they made mistakes or didn't work hard enough, Mr. Bumble beat them.

At mealtimes, the boys were given a bowl of thin porridge, known as "gruel." They grew thinner and thinner, hungrier and hungrier. Oliver feared that one of the bigger boys was hungry enough to eat *him*!

They decided they must do something or starve to death. One of them would tell the cook what they all wanted. They drew lots and the boy chosen to do this was Oliver.

That evening, when every bowl of gruel had been scraped empty, Oliver got up nervously to his feet. All eyes were on him.

Very slowly, he walked to where the cook stood before a huge tub of gruel. Quietly, in his most polite voice, Oliver asked, "Please, sir, I want some more."

The greasy cook turned pale. "What?" he gasped.

"Please, sir," repeated Oliver, "I want some more."

The workhouse staff couldn't believe it. Ask for *more*? How rude! How ungrateful!

The men shouted, the women screamed, and Mr. Bumble hurried into the room. *More*?! He'd never heard anything so ridiculous in all his life. The boy had to go.

Oliver was thrashed and locked in a room for a week. The only sound was his own crying. Outside, Mr. Bumble put

 up a notice asking someone to take Oliver away and teach him a skill. He offered five pounds to whoever did this.

A cruel chimney sweep saw the notice and grinned. His last three workhouse boys had died, and he needed a new one.

He made a deal with
Mr. Bumble.

A group of
important men,
the magistrates,
had to approve
this deal. They
didn't like the

way the chimney sweep behaved—he sent
boys up the inside of chimneys to clean
them. If they got stuck, he lit a fire to
drive them out!

Did Oliver want to be a chimney
sweep, they asked. "No!" he wept,
unable to lie. "Please starve me or even
kill me—but don't send me with that
dreadful man!"

Oliver did not become a chimney
sweep, but Mr. Bumble did beat him again.

Can you imagine poor Oliver? He was small, thin, and pale, with such a sad look on his little face! Who would want a boy like that? Well, there was one person—Mr. Sowerberry.

Mr. Sowerberry was an undertaker. He collected the bodies of people who had died. He then made their coffins and arranged their funerals. He needed someone to walk beside children's coffins. This person had to be small and look truly sad.

When Mr. Bumble showed Oliver to Mr. Sowerberry, the undertaker rubbed his hands. Just the boy he needed!

The two men had a chat, and Oliver left the workhouse to live with Mr. and Mrs. Sowerberry and their daughter Charlotte.

Mr. Bumble was delighted to get rid of
Oliver. The Sowerberrys were delighted to
find such a miserable-looking boy. Only
Oliver was unhappy. He had been sold,
like a carpet or a kettle. Nobody loved
him; nobody had ever loved him.

Mr. Sowerberry was quite kind to
Oliver, but Mrs. Sowerberry grumbled
at him for eating too much. Charlotte's
boyfriend, Noah Claypole, was worse.
Every time he saw Oliver, he bullied him.
One day, he went too far.

At dinner time, Noah pulled Oliver's hair and twisted his ears. Oliver, who had a heart of gold, did nothing, which annoyed Noah. "Hey, workhouse boy," he said, "how's your mother?"

"She's dead," replied Oliver. "Don't you dare say anything bad about her!"

"What did she die of, workhouse boy?"

"She died of a broken heart," replied Oliver quietly. A tear rolled down his cheek.

"Oh, dear," sneered Noah. "I'll tell you what, she was a right bad one!"

"What did you say?" whispered Oliver.

"I said she was a right bad one!"

Oliver exploded with anger and punched Noah with all his strength. The bully fell flat on the floor, crying. Mrs. Sowerberry hurried in, and she and Charlotte attacked Oliver.

As the two women scratched and punched the poor boy, Noah ran to fetch Mr. Bumble. "Oliver Twist tried to murder me!" he lied.

Mr. Bumble hurried to the Sowerberrys'. The problem was meat, he said. They should never have given Oliver meat.

When he heard this, Mr. Sowerberry beat Oliver soundly. Mr. Bumble did the same. Finally, battered and bruised, the orphan boy was sent to his lonely bed.

CHAPTER 2
Into the Den of Thieves

Oliver was very brave while Mr. Bumble and the Sowerberrys were hurting him. He didn't cry once. But now, all alone, the bruised and unhappy little boy fell to his knees and wept.

Around the middle of the night, Oliver rose and looked outside. The night was cold and clear. *Yes*, he thought, *I will run away*!

At first light, he opened the Sowerberrys' front door and stepped outside into the fresh air. His path took him beside the workhouse. He shuddered when he saw the grim building. A young boy named Dick was already at work in the garden.

"Hello, Dick," said Oliver quietly. "Please don't tell anyone you saw me.

I'm running away."

Dick looked pale and sad. "I wish I could come with you, Oliver," he said with a sob. "But the doctor says I'm dying."

Oliver came up to the iron bars of the garden fence. Dick stretched out his thin arms and held on to him. "Don't stop, dear Oliver," he said kindly. "Goodbye, and God bless you!"

This was the first time anyone had said that to Oliver, and he never once forgot it.

Oliver was terrified that Mr. Bumble would come after him, and he ran until he could run no more. After that, he struggled on, step after step, for twenty miles.

Beside the road, he saw a stone with "London 70 miles" carved into it. *London—what a great place!* he thought. *No one will ever find me there. That's where I will go.*

Seventy miles is a long, long way for a small boy with no food and nothing to drink. Oliver was about to collapse on the road, like his dear mother, when a kindly old couple took pity on him. They invited him in and gave him a large meal.

Refreshed, Oliver struggled on to the town of Barnet. He had now been walking for seven days, and his feet were terribly sore. He was starving hungry again, too. He sat down in despair.

"Hello!" said a voice.

Oliver looked up at the strangest person he had ever seen. He was about Oliver's age, but he behaved and spoke like an adult. He wore a man's coat, with the sleeves rolled up. On his head sat a top hat, always about to fall off.

"Hello," repeated the stranger. "What are you up to, then?"

"I'm tired and starving hungry," replied Oliver. He was trying hard not to cry. "I've been walking for seven days."

"Running away from the beak, I suppose?" said the stranger. He looked closely at Oliver. "Know what a beak is?"

"Yes," said Oliver. "It's a bird's mouth."

The stranger laughed. "Maybe. But in my world a 'beak' is a magistrate." He put his hands in his pockets, and asked, "Got any money?"

"No," replied Oliver.

"Anything to eat? Anywhere to live?"

"No!"

"Then I'm your man!" The stranger introduced himself: Jack Dawkins, known to his friends as the Artful Dodger. He gave Oliver a hearty meal at an inn. Dodger then invited Oliver to come to

London with him and his friend, Charley.

"Shall we go now?" Oliver asked.

"Best go after dark," he replied, winking at his friend Charley.

"And where shall we stay?"

"I've a friend," said Dodger, "a very kind old gentleman who'd love to give you accommodation. Free."

"How kind of him!" smiled Oliver.

"Oh, yeah!" said Dodger and Charley together. "He's so kind."

After dark, the three boys entered London. They avoided the nice areas and tramped down muddy lanes between ugly houses. Foul smells hung in the filthy air.

Oliver was thinking of running away again, when Dodger grabbed his arm and led him down broken steps into a grimy hovel full of grubby boys. At the end of the room, cooking sausages over an open fire, stood the "very kind old gentleman."

Tangled red hair hung down over the man's thin and ugly face. He wore no shirt, only a greasy gown that reached to his dirty ankles. His name, said Dodger, was Fagin.

Fagin looked Oliver up and down. "Very glad to see you, Oliver. Very," he said. "We need good-looking lads like you, don't we, boys?"

"Yeah!" grinned the others in the room.

Oliver looked at the precious silk handkerchiefs hanging from a line. "Very pretty, aren't they, Oliver dear?" said Fagin.

Oliver nodded. The boys laughed.

Early the next morning, when he thought no one was looking, Fagin took out a box stuffed with watches, rings, and other valuables. Oliver, who was awake, stared in amazement. *How could poor people afford such beautiful things?* he wondered.

I think you know what was going on, don't you? Fagin was a thief, and his boys were a gang of pickpockets. They had stolen all those beautiful things from other people.

As we know, Oliver saw only the good in people. Dodger and Fagin had rescued him and had given him food and shelter. For this, he was most grateful. He was too innocent to notice that he was in a den of thieves—but he would soon learn the horrible truth.

When Fagin taught Oliver how to pick-pocket, he thought it was a game. After a couple of weeks, Dodger and Charley took him out "to work" with them. He was delighted to get out of Fagin's smoky den.

They wandered through the London streets, looking for a target. Dodger pointed

to a kindly looking gentleman in a green coat outside a bookshop. Oliver watched, horrified, as Dodger snatched a bright silk handkerchief from the man's pocket.

The man reached into his pocket … No handkerchief!

"Stop, thief!" he cried.

Dodger and Charley had already run away. When all eyes turned on Oliver, he, too, ran. He did not get far. A huge fist crashed into his face, and all went black.

CHAPTER 3

Escape and Recapture

Oliver didn't know why he had run when Dodger stole the silk handkerchief. Maybe because he was shocked and frightened? Whatever the reason, everyone thought he was the thief.

A policeman took Oliver before a magistrate, Mr. Fang. The terrified boy turned very pale. He was clearly sick. He couldn't even open his mouth to tell Fang his name. Moments later, he fainted.

"He's pretending," snapped Fang. "He won't get pity from me. Instead, he'll spend three months in prison doing hard work."

All this time, the gentleman in the green coat had been looking closely at Oliver. He felt sorry for the boy. What was more,

Oliver's face reminded him of someone.

"My name is Mr. Brownlow," he said to Fang. "I believe this boy isn't the thief!"

The man who owned the bookshop spoke up. He had seen everything. Two other boys had stolen the handkerchief!

At this, Mr. Brownlow asked to take Oliver home and look after him.

"All right," said Fang. "Case over!"

Just by chance, for the first time in his life, Oliver was about to discover the meaning of happiness.

Oliver was extremely unwell. He lay tucked up in bed in Mr. Brownlow's home for many days. All the while, Mrs. Bedwin, Mr. Brownlow's kindly housekeeper, nursed him like an angel.

Mr. Brownlow was very fond of Oliver—and fascinated by him. *The boy looks like the portrait of the pretty young woman which hangs in my house,* he thought. *When he's stronger, I must ask about his family.*

Oliver also noticed the portrait. "It's strange, dear Mrs. Bedwin," he said. "I feel so close to that lovely lady. It's as if she were my mo…" He did not finish the sentence because it sounded foolish.

What a happy time Oliver spent at Mr. Brownlow's! He was well fed, slept in a clean, comfortable bed, and was taught to read and write. Above all, everyone around him was warm and kind.

*

In Fagin's den, nothing was warm or kind. The old crook was furious when he heard about Oliver. "You fools!" he hissed at Dodger and Charley. "How could you lose him? He'll now tell the police all about us—who we are and where we live."

Fagin paced around his filthy room. "We must get him back," he muttered.

Oliver was enormously grateful to Mr. Brownlow and Mrs. Bedwin. Their kindness did not spoil him because he remembered the misery of his old life. He was sad only because he couldn't repay them.

"Is there anything I can do for you?" he asked every day. The answer was always the same: "No, but thank you for asking, Oliver."

One evening, the answer was different. "Yes, there is something, Oliver," said Mr. Brownlow. "Please run down to the bookshop and return these books, and pay the man what I owe him."

Oliver was delighted. He put Mr. Brownlow's five-pound note

in his pocket, tucked the books under his arm, and went out.

Fagin had plotted with the thug Bill Sykes to recapture Oliver. Sykes got his girlfriend, Nancy, to play a cruel trick.

"Oh, my dear brother!" Nancy sobbed when she saw Oliver. "Please come home!" She threw her arms around him.

"Don't!" cried Oliver. "Who are you?"

Bystanders sided with Nancy and called Oliver an "ungrateful brute."

Bill Sykes strode up. "Books?" he shouted, grabbing those Oliver was carrying. "I told you not to steal books!"

Oliver's cries echoed into the darkness as he was dragged back to Fagin's den.

The thieves took Oliver's fine clothes. Sykes ripped up his books, and Fagin grabbed his five-pound note. Sykes snatched it from him, saying it was his pay for recapturing the boy.

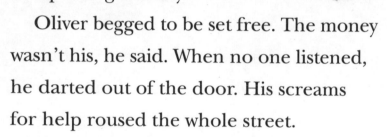

Oliver begged to be set free. The money wasn't his, he said. When no one listened, he darted out of the door. His screams for help roused the whole street.

Dodger and Charley dragged Oliver back into the dark room. Fagin raised a heavy club.

"So, you wanted to get away, my dear, did you?" he said.

Oliver did not reply.

"Called for the police, did you?" sneered Fagin. "Well, take that!" He crashed the club onto Oliver's shoulders.

Before he could strike again, Nancy threw herself forward. "Stop! You got the boy, Fagin. Isn't that enough?"

Fagin and Sykes told her to be quiet, but she refused. Yes, she lived a life of crime, she said. But she knew good from evil. For once, she would do the right thing: She'd defend innocent Oliver against them all.

Oliver was not beaten any longer, just locked in a dark room. As he lay

down to sleep, he knew that, even in Fagin's foul den, he had found one good person: Nancy.

While Oliver was Fagin's prisoner, Mr. Bumble came to London. There he saw a notice put up by Mr. Brownlow. It offered a reward for information about a boy named Oliver Twist.

Mr. Bumble wanted the money. He told Mr. Brownlow and Mrs. Bedwin that Oliver was a lying, low-born rascal. Since they loved Oliver, they didn't believe him.

Meanwhile, a mysterious man named Monks was also looking for Oliver. After finding him, Monks offered Fagin money to turn Oliver into a criminal.

Fagin set to work. Every day, he told Oliver that robbing was an amusing game. In the end, Oliver began to believe this.

Monks's plot was now ready. Bill Sykes needed a boy to help him rob a house. He had to be small enough to squeeze through a tiny window, open the front door, and let in the robbers. Oliver was just the right size.

Nancy had to bring Oliver to Bill Sykes. She didn't want to, because she loved Oliver and knew he had a good heart. But, terrified of her brutal boyfriend, she did as she was ordered.

Thus, one dark and gloomy night, poor little Oliver Twist became a thief.

CHAPTER 4

The Mystery of Oliver Twist

Sykes pushed Oliver through the tiny window in the house he was robbing.

"Now, open the front door, and let me in," growled the thug. "And remember my pistol. One false step, and I'll shoot!"

Sykes didn't shoot Oliver, but someone in the house did. Hearing a noise downstairs, they grabbed a gun. Bang! Oliver staggered, blood pouring from his

arm. Sykes grabbed him by the collar and heaved him back through the window. He carried Oliver until he heard men coming after him. To get away quicker, he dropped Oliver into a ditch and ran off.

More dead than alive, Oliver crawled toward the nearest light. It came from the house where he had been shot! On the doorstep, he collapsed, and passed out.

In the house lived a pretty girl named Rose and her good-hearted guardian, Mrs. Maylie. When they that saw Oliver was badly wounded and likely to die, they took pity on him. They paid for a doctor to treat him and informed the police the boy had nothing to do with the break-in.

In the care of these good people, Oliver recovered. Once again, he enjoyed the comfort of a loving, peaceful home.

When Oliver didn't return, Fagin visited Nancy. She said Sykes was still gone, too.

"It's my fault," she wailed. "Poor little Oliver! I should never have helped make him into a robber."

"Pah!" sneered Fagin. "He's only a boy. But it's a shame. His robbing could have earned me money!"

Nancy called him a hard-hearted monster. He called her a soft-hearted fool and left.

Oliver knew nothing of his parents, but

Monks did. That's why he'd struck the bargain with Fagin.

When Fagin called on Monks, he found him furious that the robbery had gone wrong. He hated Oliver, he muttered, and needed him out of the way. Once again, he explained his plan to Fagin.

"I pay you to make Oliver a criminal, right?" Monks began. "The boy commits a crime, and the police arrest him. The judge sends him to Australia, where criminals go these days. And Oliver Twist disappears forever!"

Why did he want this? Because he and Oliver were brothers! Their father had left them money. With Oliver gone, he would have it all to himself!

Do you remember, at the beginning of our story, how a locket and a ring were stolen from Oliver's mother? It happened in the workhouse, moments after she died.

Oliver believed his mother had left him nothing. If he found the stolen jewels, he would learn who his mother was. But Monks didn't want Oliver to know about his parents. He was determined to find the ring and the locket and destroy them.

Widow Corney, a nurse at the workhouse, knew about the things stolen

from Oliver's mother. She also liked the fat and important Mr. Bumble. And he liked the well-off Widow Corney.

After smiling at each other for a time, the pair were married.

It was not a happy marriage. Widow Corney wanted everything her own way. If Mr. Bumble disagreed, she screamed at him. After a while, he wished he had never married.

After one of his fights with his wife,

 Mr. Bumble went to the pub. Monks was waiting for him.

"I think you can get something for me," whispered Monks. "I will pay good money for it."

Mr. Bumble asked what Monks wanted. When Monks said he wanted the stolen locket and ring, Mr. Bumble smiled.

Monks met with Mr. Bumble and Widow Corney at night, in a building resting on poles over a black, muddy river.

"We're here," announced Mr. Bumble. He didn't know which he was more afraid of, his wife or Monks.

"Give me the things," snarled Monks.

"Money first!" said Mr. Bumble.

"Twenty pounds," snapped Monks.

"Twenty-five," replied Mr. Bumble.

Monks agreed. He handed over the money, and Widow Corney gave him a small bag containing the jewels stolen from Oliver's mother.

Monks tore it open. Inside was the locket holding two strands of hair. The name "Agnes" was engraved on the gold wedding ring. Here, at last, was the name of Oliver's mother!

"What will you do with them?" asked
Widow Corney.

"You'll see," said Monks. With these
words, he opened a hatch in the floor of
the room. Below them, the river swirled
and gurgled. For a moment, Mr. Bumble
feared Monks was going to push *him*
down there. Instead, he dropped the bag
into the water. It fell with a tiny splash
and was carried away by the current.

Now the jewels were gone, Monks needed Oliver to be caught stealing. That's why Fagin had Sykes use the boy in his robbery. But it had gone wrong, and Oliver was living with Rose and Mrs. Maylie. Monks went to see Fagin to plan their next step.

The pair met in Fagin's den. He sent the boys out and told Nancy to stay where she was. Fagin and Monks then went into the next room. When they were alone, Monks told Fagin about the locket and the ring.

"The last link to Oliver's mother has gone," he chortled. "The money will all be mine. But first we must get Oliver back."

Nancy was secretly listening at the door. She heard about the locket and the ring, about Monks being Oliver's brother,

and about the plan to get Oliver sent to
Australia as a criminal!

What could she do? She ought to tell
Oliver's new friends the truth. But if she
did, she would be in danger from the
murderous Bill Sykes.

Nancy chose the path of goodness and
honesty. Knowing that Rose and Mrs.
Maylie were in London, she went to see
them to pass on what she had heard.

CHAPTER 5

Murder!

Nancy rang the doorbell of the house where Rose was staying. "We don't want girls like you in here!" said the servants.

Nancy pleaded, and eventually a kind maid showed her into Rose's sitting room. Nancy expected Rose to be snobbish like the servants. But she wasn't at all. She felt sorry for Nancy and listened carefully to her story.

"Thank you so much," she exclaimed when Nancy had finished. "You have been very kind—and very brave."

"I am only doing the right thing for little Oliver," explained Nancy.

Rose smiled at her. "Of course. And you have put yourself in danger. Why not stay here? We'll protect you from Sykes."

When Nancy said she had to get back, Rose sighed. They agreed to meet again by London Bridge. In the meantime, Rose would tell Mr. Brownlow Nancy's news.

When Rose and Oliver called on Mr. Brownlow and Mrs. Bedwin, the room was filled with hugs and kisses and tears of joy.

Afterward, Rose told Mr. Brownlow about Monks's plot. They must get hold of Oliver's wicked brother, they agreed. Nancy had promised to help.

Rose was right when she said it was dangerous for Nancy to visit her. As Nancy was getting ready for the secret meeting at London Bridge, Sykes got angry.

He frowned when she put on her hat and asked sharply, "Where are you going, Nance?"

"Nowhere important," she replied, twisting her fingers anxiously.

Sykes swore. "Then, you're not going," he ordered.

Nancy was very upset to miss the meeting. She cried and stamped her feet. Fagin noticed her mood and thought, *Aha! This girl is up to something!*

Fagin needed someone to spy on

Nancy. The boys would be too young. He wondered if he could trust the new member of his gang. In the end, he decided he could.

And who was this person? Noah Claypole! The same cruel oaf who had bullied Oliver when he worked for Mr. Sowerberry. Noah had stolen money, run away to London, and joined Fagin's gang.

"Want to do a little job for me, Noah?" Fagin asked.

"Anything you wish, Mr. Fagin, sir," replied Noah with a bow.

Fagin nodded. "You any good at spying?"

"It's what I'm best at," grinned Noah.

"Good. Then listen carefully …"

While Noah Claypole was preparing to spy on Nancy, something extraordinary happened. The Dodger was arrested!

He was not caught for stealing something valuable, but for taking a small box worth two and a half pennies! He was furious. In the law court, he made a great scene. He was a "victim," he said. The police had taken away his "privileges"!

The judge took no notice of Dodger's nonsense and ordered him to be sent to Australia. Fagin's gang was falling apart. It wouldn't be long before the police caught up with Fagin himself.

Meanwhile, Noah had set out after Nancy when she sneaked off on her own one night. He followed her through the dark streets to London Bridge. There, he hid where he could hear her conversation with Rose and Mr. Brownlow.

Nancy agreed to tell them where Monks lived. So, thought Noah, *Nancy's love for Oliver is greater than her friendship with Fagin. She is a traitor to the gang!*

Noah went straight back to Fagin and reported what he had heard. An evil look came into the old man's eyes, a look that said he would teach Nancy a lesson she would never forget!

"Bill, your Nancy is a good girl," said Fagin when he next met Bill Sykes.

The thug nodded. "Yeah, she's all right, I suppose."

"Pity she likes Oliver Twist more than us," said Fagin casually.

"What do you mean?" cried Sykes. "Speak up, you old skeleton!"

Fagin told him what Noah had overheard. He twisted the story, suggesting that Nancy would turn Sykes over to the police.

Sykes gave a terrible scowl. He frowned and ground his teeth. Swearing dreadfully, he stormed out of the room and ran to his own house.

Nancy smiled when she heard him come in. Her look changed to one of terror when she saw his face.

"Please, Bill," she begged, grabbing hold of him. "I've done you no harm!"

"No harm?" roared Sykes. "Liar!"

Nancy's face was streaked with tears. "I love you, Bill," she gasped, clinging tightly to him.

"Get off me, traitor!" he shouted, pushing her away.

He raised his pistol above his head …

When Sykes saw what he had done, he was filled with shame and horror. He had done many wicked things, but this was the worst. There could be no forgiveness, no mercy for a man who had killed an innocent girl.

Sykes could not stay in London, where everyone would guess who had killed Nancy. He fled into the countryside, where he hoped to be safe.

But there was no escape. When he tried to rest, Nancy's ghost floated before his eyes. She haunted him—and would haunt him to the end.

Wherever Sykes went, all the talk was of the cruel murder of a young woman. He felt all eyes were on him. He had nowhere to hide.

In desperation, he returned to London. He knew of a dark and dirty building where he wouldn't be found. He was wrong.

A man recognized him, and a large crowd gathered outside. "Murderer!" the mob cried. "Come out, you monster!"

The only escape was across the roof.

Sykes found a rope. On one end, he made a loop to go around his body. The other end he tied to the chimney.

Carefully, he climbed out of the window and edged along the roof.

Below, the mob bellowed and shrieked. Above, Sykes stared at the ghost of Nancy, slipped—and fell.

The rope that was supposed to go around his body went only around his neck. And that was the end of Bill Sykes.

CHAPTER 6

Happiness!

Nancy had told Rose and Mr. Brownlow what Monks looked like and where he could be found. Mr. Brownlow went there with two strong men and forced Monks to return home with him.

"Now," he said, when the two men were alone, "tell me the truth."

At first, Monks said he didn't know what Mr. Brownlow was talking about.

But when he heard what Nancy had said about him and Fagin, Monks confessed.

Monks's real name was Edward Leeford. His father, Edwin Leeford, was Mr. Brownlow's best friend. Edwin had been forced to marry a woman he didn't love, and after the birth of Edward, the couple separated. Years later, Mrs. Leeford died.

How does Oliver Twist fit into all this? Read on, and you will see …

Free from his unhappy marriage, Edwin Leeford fell in love. The girl he adored was named Agnes. One day, he told Mr. Brownlow all about the lovely Agnes, and he gave him a portrait of her. This portrait still hung in Mr. Brownlow's house.

Before marrying Agnes, Edwin tragically died. Agnes, who was expecting a baby, was left by herself with nothing.

I expect you've guessed what comes next, haven't you?

Agnes was the poor young woman who died in Mr. Bumble's workhouse at the beginning of our story. Her baby was Oliver Twist.

No wonder Mr. Brownlow thought Oliver looked like the picture hanging on his wall! Agnes was Oliver's mother. It's not surprising Oliver also loved the picture.

"Well, Edward Leeford," said Mr. Brownlow. "What did you do when you learned you had a brother?"

"I was furious," muttered Leeford. "Half my father's money would go to this wretched Oliver Twist. I wanted it all for myself—I had to get rid of him."

Mr. Brownlow looked shocked. "Get rid of him?"

"Not kill him! I wanted Fagin to make him a criminal, so he'd be sent to Australia. Like the Artful Dodger."

"And your wicked plan failed," said Mr. Brownlow, shaking his head. "Oliver has a heart of gold, and he could never be a criminal."

When Oliver heard his brother's story, he gave him a second chance. After all, Oliver said, Mr. Brownlow and Rose had both given *him* a second chance. He shared the family money between himself and his half-brother.

Edward Leeford was grateful to Oliver for sharing the family money and for his second chance. He stopped using the name "Monks." From now on, he promised, he would lead an honest life.

Promises are easier to make than keep. Edward went to America. There, he said, everyone could make money. True, he did make money, but he made it as a criminal.

He was caught and sent to prison. The man who had tried to get his hands on everything, ended up with nothing.

*

The police caught up with Fagin, too. He was found guilty of many crimes. The worst was training boys, such as Dodger and Charley Bates, to be thieves. The judge said execution was the only suitable punishment for such crimes.

Oliver and Mr. Brownlow went to see
Fagin on his last evening. They found him
sitting on the stone bed in his cell. He was
filthier than ever. His clothes were torn,
his long red hair hung over his face, his
eyes stared at things that were not there.

When Oliver asked him if he wanted
to say a prayer, Fagin mumbled nonsense.
His mind had already gone. In the
morning, his body would be gone, too.

Fagin's gang was no more. His boys were horrified to learn that Bill Sykes had murdered Nancy, and most of them gave up thieving.

The Artful Dodger's friend, Charley Bates, left London altogether. He decided to move to the countryside, where the air was cleaner and criminals did not hang about on every street corner. Charley's honest, hard work as a cattle farmer paid off, and in the end it made him a very wealthy man.

*

That leaves just two more rogues for us to learn about: Mr. Bumble and the Widow Corney. The magistrates got to hear how the locket and the ring had been stolen from Oliver's mother. They learned, too, how Mr. Bumble and the Widow Corney had sold these jewels to Monks.

For these disgraceful actions, Mr. Bumble and the Widow Corney lost their jobs. What could they do now? Mr. Bumble knew only how to eat and drink and be a bully. Widow Corney knew only how to scream, lie, and cheat. No one wanted good-for-nothings like that working for them. With no jobs, they grew poorer and poorer.

The wicked pair became so poor, in fact, that they were sent to a workhouse—the very same one where Mr. Bumble had once been the big bully. A lot of people said it served them right.

*

Oliver's story has one more surprise. The beautiful Rose, the young woman who had been so kind to him, turned out to be his mother's sister. She was his aunt!

The two of them spent many happy

hours together. Aunt and nephew walked in the countryside and chatted by the fireside. In time, Rose married her boyfriend, Harry. He was as fond of Oliver as she was. And when the couple had children, they also loved Oliver dearly.

When not visiting Rose and Harry, Oliver lived with Mr. Brownlow and Mrs. Bedwin. Because Mr. Brownlow had been such a good friend of Oliver's father, he adopted the boy. The wise and good-hearted old man did all he could for his adopted son. He gave him a good education and, most important of all, a secure and loving home.

Oliver Twist, the orphan child with a heart of gold, had entered life all alone. Though wicked people did their worst to harm him, he never gave up.

Now, Rose has taken the place of his mother, and Mr. Brownlow has taken the place of his father. And so our story, which started with tears, ends with smiles and happy laughter.